The Little Book of
NOT SO

For Luther
Little, but Not So Little in my heart

www.houghtonmifflinbooks.com

The text of this book is set in Triplex Condensed.

The illustrations are ink line drawings, digitized & colored in Photoshop.

Library of Congress Cataloging-in-Publication Data

Harper, Charise Mericle.

The little book of not so / by Charise Mericle Harper.

p. cm.

Summary: Presents a series of comparisons, such as "Big," "Not So Big" and "Tasty," "Not So Tasty" on successive pages.

ISBN 0-618-47319-x

1. English language—Adjective—Juvenile literature. 2. English language—Comparison—Juvenile literature. [1. English language—Comparison. 2. Vocabulary.] I. Title.

PE1241.H34 2005   428.1—dc22   2004009216

ISBN 13: 978-0-618-47319-9

Manufactured in China

SCP 10 9 8 7 6 5 4 3 2 1

The Little Book of
NOT SO

CHARISE MERICLE HARPER

Houghton Mifflin Company Boston 2005

GOOD

Not So **Good**

HIGH

Not So **High**

BIG

Not So **Big**

PRETTY

Not So **Pretty**

DARK

Not So **Dark**

SCARY

Not So **Scary**

TASTY

Not So **Tasty**

MANY

Not So **Many**

LOUD

Not So **Loud**

LONELY

Not So **Lonely**

SAFE

Not So **Safe**

WET

Not So **Wet**

FRIENDLY

Not So **Friendly**

SLEEPY

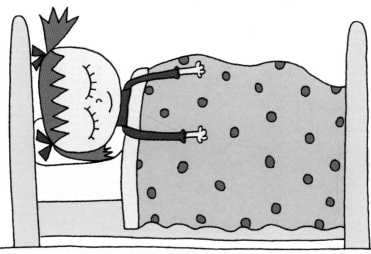

Not So **Sleepy**